THE TRAIN RIDE

S0-ANG-407

written by J. David Loeb

illustrated by Brad A. Steventon

Otter Creek
PUBLISHING COMPANY
MULVANE, KANSAS

The Otter Creek Publishing Company, of Mulvane, Kansas, was established to produce children's books written and illustrated by Kansas authors and artists. The stories and art work do not just depict Kansas, but vary in content for nationwide appeal. It is hoped that the children of Kansas will see and read our books, with the realization of the opportunity they possess as future authors and artists - right in their home state.

Copyright © 1994 by Otter Creek Publishing Company. All rights reserved. No part of this book may be reproduced or copied in any form or by any means, without prior written permission of the publisher. Printed in the U.S.A. Published by Otter Creek Publishing Company, R.R. 1, Box 327, Mulvane, Kansas 67110.

ISBN: 1-885744-02-1

Come along and ride with me,
I'm the old engineer.
I'd really like to show you,
Sights I enjoy each year.

Do you see the oil well rigs?
Monsters pecking the ground!
They're pumping deep in the earth,
Where precious oil is found.

See all the black clouds forming?
We'll hear the frightening sound,
Of mighty claps of thunder,
When lightning strikes the ground.

There is a pretty rainbow,
Arched wide across the sky.
It's made by rain and sunshine,
As the storm passes by.

See, there's a little bluebird,
Just darting through the trees.
They sway so soft and gently,
In the warm summer breeze.

That's a flock of wild turkeys,
Sixty birds, maybe more.
They are the birds made famous,
By early pilgrim's lore.

Quick! Look at the running deer.
He heard the whistle scream.
He ran right through the buck brush,
And jumped a little stream.

The bright full moon is shining,
Flooding the land with light.
It's a pretty scene to see,
Riding the train at night.

Do you see the small red fox,
Running across the land?
She is going to her den,
Which must be close at hand.

Can you see the Big Dipper?
It points to the North Star.
It's a huge constellation,
That tells us where we are.

Look, there goes a shooting star!
It's blazing through the night.
It lived for just a moment,
And now it's gone from sight.

See the little prairie dogs,
They live there in a town,
Underneath the mounds of earth,
Where they have burrowed down.

When you look across the fields,
You will see, just by chance,
Those five whirling dust devils,
Doing their spinning dance.

Here come the waving children!
I often wonder why,
They like this old train so much,
As it goes rolling by.

That's a field of sunflowers,
Rooted deep in the soil.
They'll be reaped in the autumn,
For wholesome seeds and oil.

The symbol of our freedom,
Is flying wild and free.
It is the mighty eagle,
Which we're so proud to see.

Look at the silent bobcat,
He ran across the track!
He can run all through the woods,
And not a twig will crack.

You see the ring-necked pheasant,
Fly, then light on the ground?
Soon he'll run away to hide,
In hopes he won't be found.

The trees have many colors,
We know that things are grand,
When we see trees in autumn,
Painted by nature's hand.

Notice how Mother Nature,
Covers the earth with snow,
Just broken by the river,
Where running waters flow.

Listen! Hear the wild geese honk?
They fly a perfect vee.
It means spring will soon be here,
A thrilling sight to see!

Well now, all you boys and girls,
I hope you liked our ride.
As we traveled together,
Around the countryside.